D1596514

Pasó Por Aquí

THE WESTERN FRONTIER LIBRARY

PASÓ POR AQUÍ

By
Eugene Manlove Rhodes

WITH AN INTRODUCTION BY
W. H. Hutchinson

AND ILLUSTRATIONS BY
W. H. D. Koerner

UNIVERSITY OF OKLAHOMA PRESS

NORMAN

Library of Congress Cataloging in Publication Data

Rhodes, Eugene Manlove, 1869–1934.
    Pasó por aquí.

    (The Western frontier library, v. 50)
    I. Title.
PZ3.R3443Pas5   813'.5'2   72–9273

Con Razón

By W. H. Hutchinson

When it graced the *Saturday Evening Post*, February 2–27, 1926, "Pasó Por Aquí" made only Rhodes's second remunerative publication in almost six years, and was itself almost a year later than "Once in the Saddle" which had broken his productive drought. Four more dry years would elapse before Rhodes made another major appearance in print. That *Saturday Evening Post* took what Rhodes wrote whenever he wrote it is a tribute to what he had to offer, because the *Post*'s fiction contributors in this period of its heyday were expected to appear regularly within its covers.

Houghton Mifflin Company, his book publishers, had not had a book from Rhodes since 1922. In response to his importunities and his exemption from royalty of the first thousand copies to be sold, they published these two novellas together in 1927 as *Once in the Saddle*. The effort went almost for nought. It had the smallest sale of any of Rhodes's books, less than 3,000 copies, and suffered the indignity of being remaindered in Canada below cost. It was, as well, the only one of Rhodes's books not reprinted in England or in an inexpensive edition in the United States.

A similar dubious distinction attached itself to "Pasó Por Aquí" in 1948, when it became the last of Rhodes's works to be transferred to film. As "Four Faces West," it featured Joel McCrea as *Ross McEwen*, Charles Bickford as *Pat Garrett*, and Frances Dee as *Jay Hollister*. Much of the picture was shot on location where the story had been laid, which titivated the citizens of Alamogordo, stimulated their community's economy, and gave it coveted publicity.

The film was produced as an independent

venture by Harry "Pops" Sherman, a veteran and eminently successful maker of "B" Westerns. According to a filmland contemporary:

> . . . in his old age he wanted to make a "fine" western. He made it. I personally liked the picture very much but the thing laid the biggest egg ever laid by any picture ever made in this business. It cost well over a million to make and . . . withdrew the picture from circulation, a thing that has happened only once or twice [*sic*] in all the history of Hollywood. Harry made the fatal mistake of doing an intelligent western, with not one shot fired, not even a fist fight.

Professor James K. Folsom, an astute student of horse opera in all its mutant forms, has expressed a divergent view of the film: "Basically a pot boiler and pretty much ruins the novelette." Television's insatiable maw gave "Four Faces West" a reprieve from oblivion, as personal experience recalls it making the late, late, LATE! program on several stations well into the past decade.

"After the spur, corn!," as our folk-say once

would have described what follows. "Pasó Por Aquí" is the most anthologized of any of Rhodes's stories and is among the most anthologized of any so-called "Western story." A recent (1971) poll of members of Western Writers of America concerning outstanding fiction and non-fiction of the West-That-Was brought it substantial votes from these riders of the typewriter range, including the comment by one respondent that it was "the finest western ever written."

The literary and academic *cognoscenti* of our parlous present have not overlooked "Pasó Por Aquí" in their unceasing quest for parapsychological pulsations from the vanished West. Some have seen it as a somber and elegiac lament for an ungelded freedom. To others, it has been the casting-out from the Garden by the machine called civilization. Still others have seen it as a flaming statement of Western egalitarian populist protest against the exploiting and elitist East. And the fleeing outlaw who succors a diphtheria-stricken Hispañic family has been heralded as a stinging rebuke to middle-class Anglo racism. There is merit as well as clotted nonsense among these views, none of which, for an opinion, reach to the heart of the story.

There is more of Rhodes, "that hard-bitten master of simplicity" as Stanley Walker dubbed him, in this story than in any of his others. More of the man himself; more of his importunate spirit; more of his passionate commitment to the *ethos* of the oasis community of his youth and young manhood that gave all his life its deepest meaning.

While Rhodes himself never had played Good Samaritan to a diphtheria-stricken, isolated family, he had been a *volunteer* nurse in a diphtheria pest house in a day when that was a dread disease indeed. Those moderns who say that Rhodes took the hazard of diphtheria from a much older time in the West's history have not enjoyed this writer's experience with it in Ranger, Texas, in 1919.

"The greatest ox ride in the annals of the cow country was made and will keep on being made

by the cowboy-outlaw-cavalier Ross McEwen,"
so said J. Frank Dobie. Just so did Rhodes in
life.

> I rode that steer myself—a brindle steer with
> big horns. And that is exactly how-come I know
> how to do it. Seven miles I made before he sulled
> [sulked] on me. I wasn't particular where I
> went, you see, or he might have sulled sooner.
> Where I wanted to go was AWAY!

The route of McEwen's flight is described
from life, for Rhodes rode that very route himself and for similar reason. He had not robbed
a merchant—although the flourishing folklore
about him holds that he once robbed a bank—
but he had won an argument with the Sheriff
of Socorro County, who was ex-officio tax col-
lector, over the amount, time, and method of
collection of taxes on Rhodes's ranch and live-
stock. The damage to the Sheriff's *amour-propre*
had caused him to give chase in the interests of
re-election, but Rhodes reached the friendly con-
fines of Otero County, where Socorro writs did
not run, ahead of him.

Pasó Por Aquí

Patrick Floyd Garrett, a towering figure in our Powdersmoke Pantheon, never was Sheriff of Otero County, as he is in this story. However, he had been Sheriff of Dona Aña County at a time when two men he sought most vigorously, Oliver Milton Lee and James Gililland, had had no more hot-eyed partisan than Rhodes. Thus, for several years, Garrett and Rhodes had been bitter enemies. Garrett's role in this story was Rhodes's means of refuting what he felt had been an unconscionable maligning of Garrett by Walter Noble Burns in the latter's *Saga of Billy The Kid*.

Explicit in his use of *Rosalio Marquez*, called "Monte" from his profession, is what Rhodes had learned and never forgotten: In the oasis community of his formative years, it mattered not the color of a man's skin nor the manner in which he earned his living when it came down in life to the nut-cutting stage. "Monte was an old friend," he later wrote, "and he died in Alamogordo just a week before I returned after a twenty-year absence."

He had learned this lesson from Francisco Bojórquez, wagon boss for the J-Half Circle-Cross when that iron marked 30,000 head of cattle, a man for whom the chalk-eyed, pigment-proud Texians who made up his crew were proud to work. He had learned it from José and Felipe Lucero, who were Dona Aña County's sheriff turn-and-turn about for many years. He had learned it from Elfego Baca, a notable *pistolero* and *jefe político* in a notably corrupt town, Socorro. And he had learned it from Anastacio Barela, who first wounded Rhodes with his .45 and then almost pistol-whipped him into extinction one night in Old Mesilla. What he had learned, he later wrote: "This is a conquered race—and a proud and sensitive race when you take'em where they were born and raised. They may forgive you for taking a shot or two at them—but *never* for high hatting 'em." It is to *Monte*, for due cause, that Rhodes entrusts the task of explaining the continuity of the generations in their land to the Outlander from the East.

Rhodes made more skillful use of the East-
erner in this story than in any other, although
he used Easterners, either as villains or as ve-
hicles for explaining the customs and artifacts
of the tawny, western barbarians, from the be-
ginning of his writing career to its end. Rhodes
knew, long before it became an article of faith
among political scientists and historians, that
his West had been and was the exploited prov-
ince of the financial, commercial, and political
East. He protested against this many times with
wild jackassian brays. In this story, he strove
mightily to show that the East's social and literary pretensions to superiority were the height
of egregious asininity.

He resented the then-current cliché, which
persists today, that made the West, his "ain
countree," the symbol of wasteland. He knew
that courage and humor and loyalties and sym-
pathies were what had held society together in
the vast, oasis-dotted regions of his youth, just
as these qualities had held society together "on
Hudson's pampas, in Barrie's Thrums, in Ak-

sakoff's old Russia, on Rassul Galwan's Tibetan plateau." His people had lived active lives, objective lives, productive lives; asking little and enduring much. They had settled the problems of right and wrong without Freud and without blaming society. They *were* society!

In "Pasó Por Aquí" he wrote about them with wit and gusto and tenderness; with probity and clarity and a sureness of interpretation as yet unequaled. In so doing, he captured for all time the free, lonely, self-reliant, skilled, eternally optimistic essence of his West and of the nation, in his view, that the West had built.

California State University, Chico

Illustrations

The illustrations in this edition of Pasó Por Aquí are by W. H. D. Koerner (1878–1938) and are reproduced here through the courtesy of Ruth Koerner Oliver.

"The pursuing dust did not come fast,
   but it came straight his way."   *pages* 40–41

"He heard a choking cough, a child's
   wailing cry. His foot was on the
   threshold. 'What's wrong?
   Que es?' he called."   78–79

"He sat by that door, where he could
   see into the sick room. They were
   all asleep."   86–87

"That is how they came to Lost Ranch
   between three and four the
   next morning."   104–105

Pasó Por Aquí

EXCEPTIONS are so inevitable that no rule is without them—except the one just stated. Neglecting fractions then, not to insult intelligence by specifying the obvious, trained nurses are efficient, skillful, devoted. It is a noble calling. Nevertheless, it is notorious that the official uniform is of reprehensible charm. This regulation is variously explained by men, women, and doctors. "No fripperies, curlicues, and didos—bully!" say the men. "Ah! Yes! But why? Artful minxes!" say the women, who should know best. "Cheerful influence in the sick room," say the doctors.

Be that as it may, such uniform Jay wore,

spotless and starched, crisp and cool; Jay Hollister, now seated on the wide portico of the Alamogordo Hospital; not chief nurse, but chief ornament, according to many, not only of that hospital, but also of the great railroad which maintained it. Alamogordo was a railroad town, a new town, a ready-made and highly painted town, direct from Toyland.

Ben Griggs was also a study in white—flannels, oxfords, and panama; a privileged visitor who rather overstepped his privileges; almost a fixture in that pleasant colonnade.

"Lamp of life," said Ben, "let's get down to brass tacks. You're homesick!"

"Homesick!" said Jay scornfully. *"Homesick! I'm heartsick, bankrupt, shipwrecked, lost, forlorn—here in this terrible country, among these dreadful people. Homesick? Why, Ben, I'm just damned!"

"Never mind, heart's delight—you've got me."

Miss Hollister seemed in no way soothed by this reassuring statement.

4

"Your precious New Mexico! Sand!" she said. "Sand, snakes, scorpions; wind, dust, glare, and heat; lonely, desolate, and forlorn!"

"Under the circumstances," said Ben, "you could hardly pay me a greater compliment, 'Whither thou goest, I will go,' and all that. Good girl! This unsolicited tribute——"

"Don't be a poor simpleton," advised the good girl. "I shall stick it out for my year, of course, since I was foolish enough to undertake it. That is all. Don't you make any mistakes. These people shall never be my people."

"No better people on earth. In all the essentials——"

"Oh, who cares anything about essentials?" cried Jay impatiently—voicing, perhaps, more than she knew. "A tin plate will do well enough to eat out of, certainly, if that is what you mean. I prefer china, myself. I'm going back where I can see flowers and the green grass, old gardens and sundials."

"I know not what others may say," observed Ben grandly, "but as for me, you take the sun-

5

dials and give me the sun. Right here, too, where they climb for water and dig for wood. Peevish, my fellow townsman; peevish, waspy, crabbed. You haven't half enough to do. In this beastly climate people simply will not stay sick. They take up their bed and beat it, and you can't help yourself. Nursing is a mere sinecure." His hands were clasped behind his head, his slim length reclined in a steamer chair, feet crossed, eyes half closed, luxurious. "Ah, idleness!" he murmured. "Too bad, too bad! You never were a grouch back home. Rather good company, if anything."

Ben's eyes were blue and dreamy. They opened a trifle wider now, and rolled slowly till they fell upon Miss Hollister, both upright and haughty in her chair, her lips pressed to a straight line. She regarded him sternly. He blinked, his hands came from behind his head, he straightened up and adjusted his finger-tips to meet with delicate precision. "But the main trouble, the fount and origin of your disappointing conduct is, as hereinbefore said, homesickness. It is, as has been observed, a nobler pang than indigestion, though the symptoms are of striking similarity. Nostalgia, more than any other feeling, is fatal to the judicial faculties, and I think," said Ben, "I think, my dear towny, that when you look at this fair land, your future home, you regard all things with a jaundiced eye."

"Oh-h!" gasped Jay, hotly indignant. "Look at it yourself! Look at it!"

The hospital was guarded and overhung by an outer colonnade of cottonwoods; she looked through a green archway across the leagues of shimmering desert, somber, wavering, and dim; she saw the long bleak range beyond, saw-toothed and gray; saw in the midway levels the unbearable brilliance of the White Sands, a dazzle and tumult of wild light, a blinding mirror with two score miles for diameter.

But Ben's eyes widened with delight, their blue darkened to a deeper blue of exultation, not to be feigned.

"More than beautiful—fascinating," he said.

7

"Repulsive, hateful, malignant, appalling!" cried Jay Hollister bitterly. "The starved, withered grass, the parched earth, the stunted bushes —miserable, hideous—the abomination of desolation!"

"Girl, by all good rights I ought to shut your wild, wild mouth with kisses four—that's what I orter do—elocutin' that way. But you mean it, I guess." Ben nodded his head sagely. "I get your idea. Blotched and leprous, eh? Thin, starved soil, poisoned and mildewed patches— thorns and dwarfed scrub, red leer of the sun. Oh, *si!* Like that bird in Browning? Hills like giants at a huntin' lay—the round squat turret— all the lost adventurers, my peers—the Dark Tower, weird noises just offstage, increasin' like a bill, I mean a bell—increasin' like a bell, fiddles a-moanin', 'O-o-o-h-h-h! What did you do-o-o with your summer's wa-a-a-ges? So this is Paris!' Yes, yes! But why not shed the second-hand stuff and come down to workaday?"

"Ben Griggs," said Miss Hollister with quiet and deadly conviction, "you are absolutely the most blasphemous wretch that ever walked in shoe leather. You haven't anything even remotely corresponding to a soul."

"When we are married," said Ben, and paused, reflecting. "That is, if I don't change my mind————"

"Married!" said Miss Hollister derisively. *"When! You!"* Her eyes scorned him.

"Woman," said Ben, "beware! You make utter confusion with the parts of speech. You make mere interjections of pronouns, prepositions, and verbs and everything. You use too many shockers. More than that—mark me, my lass—isn't it curious that no one has ever thought to furnish printed words with every phonograph record of a song? Just a little sheet of paper—why, it needn't cost more than a penny apiece at the outside. Then we could know what it was all about."

"The way you hop from conversational crag to crag," said Jay, "is beyond all praise."

"Oh, well, if you insist, we can go back to our marriage again."

9

"My poor misguided young friend," said Jay, "make no mistakes. I put up with you because we played together when we were kids, and because we are strangers here in a strange land, townies together———"

Ben interrupted her. "Two tawny townies twisting twill together!" he chanted happily, beating slow time with a gentle finger. "Twin turtles twitter tender twilight twaddle. Twice twenty travelers———"

"Preposterous imbecile!" said Jay, dimpling nevertheless, adorably. "Here is something to put in your little book. Jay Hollister will never marry an idler and a wastrel. Why, you're not even a ne'er-do-well. You're a do-nothing, net."

"All the world loves a loafer," Ben protested. "Still, as Alice remarked, if circumstances were different they would be quite otherwise. If frugal industry———"

"There comes your gambler friend," said Jay coldly.

"Who, Monte? Where?" Ben turned eagerly.

"Across the street. No, the other way."

Though she fervently disapproved of Monte, Jay was not sorry for the diversion. It was daily more difficult to keep Ben in his proper place, and she had no desire to discuss frugal industry.

"Picturesque rascal, what? Looking real pleased about something, too. Say, girl, you've made me forget something I was going to tell you."

"He is laughing to himself," said Jay.

"I believe he is, at that." Ben raised his voice. "Hi, Monte! Come over and tell us the joke."

CHAPTER II

MONTE's mother had known him as Rosalio
Marquez. The overname was professional. He
dealt monte wisely but not too well. He was
nearing thirty-five, the easiest age of all; he
was slender and graceful; he wore blue serge
and a soft black hat, low-crowned and wide-
brimmed. He carried his hat in his hand as he
came up the steps. He bowed courteously to
Jay, with murmured greetings in Spanish, soft
syllables of lingering caress; he waved a friendly salute to Ben.

"Yes, indeed," said Ben. "With all my heart.
Your statement as to the beauty of the day is
correct in every particular, and it affords me

great pleasure to endorse an opinion so just. But, after all, dear heart, that is hardly the point, is it? The giddy jest, the merry chuckles —those are the points on which we greatly desire information."

Monte hesitated, almost imperceptibly, a shrewd questioning in his eyes.

"Yes, have a chair," said Jay, "and tell us the joke."

"Thees is good, here, thank you," said Monte. He sat on the top step and hung the black hat on his knee; his face lit up with soft low laughter. "The joke? O, eet ees upon the sheriff, Jeem Hunter. I weel tell it."

He paused to consider. In his own tongue Monte's speech sounded uncommonly like a pack of firecrackers lit at both ends. In English it was leisured, low, and thoughtful. The unslurred vowels, stressed and piquant, the crisp consonants, the tongue-tip accents—these things combined to make the slow caressing words into something rich and colorful and strange, all unlike our own smudged and neutral speech. The customary medium of the Southwest between the two races is a weird and lawless hodge-podge of the two tongues —a barbarous *lingua franca.*

As Miss Hollister had no Spanish, Monte drew only from his slender stock of English; and all unconsciously he acted the story as he told it.

"When Jeem was a leetle, small boy," said Monte, his hand knee-high to show the size in question, "he dream manee times that he find thoss marbles—oh, many marbles! That mek heem ver' glad, thees nize dream. Then he get older"—Monte's hand rose with the sheriff's maturity—"and some time he dream of find money lak thoss marble. And now Jeem ees grown and sheriff—an' las' night he come home ver' late, ver' esleepy. I weel tell you now how eet ees, but Jeem he did not know eet. You see, Melquiades he have a leetle, litla game." He glanced obliquely at Miss Hollister, his shoulders and down-drawn lips expressed apology for the little game, and tolerance for it. "Just neeckles and dimes. An' some fellow he go home weener, and there ees hole een hees pocket. But Jeem he do not know. *Bueno*, Jeem has been to Tularosa, Mescalero, Fresnal, all places, to leef word to look out for thees fellow las' week what rob the bank at Belen, and he arrive back on a freight train las' night, mebbe so about three in the morning—oh, veree tired, ver' esleepy. So when he go up the street een the moonlight he see there a long streeng of neeckles and dimes under hees feet." Without moving, Monte showed the homeward progress of that drowsy man and his faint surprise. "So Jeem he laugh and say, 'There ees that dream again.' And he go on. But bimeby he steel see thoss neeckles, and he peench heemself, so—and he feel eet." Monte's eyes grew round with astonishment. "And he bend heemself to peek eet, and eet ees true money, and not dreaming at all. Yais. He go not back, but on ahead he peek up one dollar seexty-five cents of thees neeckles and dimes."

"I hadn't heard of any robbery, Monte," said Ben. "What about it?"

"Yes, and where is Belen?" said Jay. "Not around here, surely. I've never heard of the place."

"Oh, no, *muy lejos*—a long ways. Belen, what you call Bethlehem, ees yonder thees side of Albuquerque, a leetle. I have been there manee times, but not estraight—round about." He made a looping motion of his hand to illustrate. "Las Vegas, and then down, or by Las Cruces, and then up. Eet is hundred feefty, two hundred miles in estraight line—I do not know."

"Anybody hurt?" asked Ben.

"Oh, no—no fuss! Eet ees veree funnee. Don Numa Frenger and Don Nestor Trujillo, they have there beeg estore to sell all theengs, leetle bank, farms, esheep ranch, freighting for thoss mines, buy wool and hides—all theengs for get the monee what ees there een thees place. And las' week, maybe Friday, Saturday, Nestor he

17

ees go to deennair, and Numa Frenger ees in the estore, *solito*.

"Comes een a customer, *un colorado*—esscusa me, a red-head. He buy tomatoes, cheese, crackers, sardines, sooch things, and a nose bag, and he ask to see shotgun. Don Numa, he exheebit two, three, and thees red he peek out nize shotgun. So he ask for shells, bird-eshot, buck-eshot, and he open the buck-eshot and sleep two shells een barrel, and break eet to throw out thoss shell weeth extractor, and sleep them een again. 'Eet work fine!' he say. 'Have you canteen?'

"Then Numa Frenger he tek long pole weeth hook to get thoss canteen where eet hang from the *viga*, the r-rafter, the beams. And when he get eet, he turn around an' thees estranger ees present thees shotgun at hees meedle. Yais.

" 'Have you money een your esafe?' say the *estranjero*, the estr-ranger. And Numa ees bite hees mouth. 'Of your kindness,' say the customer, 'weel you get heem? I weel go weeth you?'

"So they get thees money from the esafe. And thees one weel not tek onlee the paper money. 'Thees gold an' seelver ees so heav-ee,' he tell Numa Frenger. 'I weel not bozzer.' Then he pay for those theengs of which he mek purchase an' correc' Don Numa when he mek meestake in the *adición*, and get hees change back. And then he say to Numa, 'Weel you not be so good to come to eshow me wheech ees best road out from thees town to the ford of the reever?' And Numa, he ees ge-nash hees teeth, but there ees no *remedio*.

"And so they go walking along thees lane between the orchards, these two togezzer, and the leetle bir-rds es-sing een the *árboles*—thees red fellow laughing and talkin' weeth Numa, ver' gay—leading hees horse by the bridle, and weeth the shotgun een the crook of hees arm. So the people loog out from the doors of their house and say, 'Ah! Don Numa ees diverrt heemself weeth hees friend."

"And when they have come beyond the town, thees fellow ees mount hees horse. 'For your courtesy,' he say, 'I thank you. At your feet,' he say. 'Weeth God!' And he ride off laughing, and een a leetle way he toss hees shotgun een a bush, and he ride on to cross the reever, eslow. But when Numa Frenger see thees, he run queeckly, although he ees a ver' fat man, an' not young; he grab thees gun, he point heem, he pull the triggle————Nozzing! He break open the gun to look wizzen side————Nozzing! *O caballeros y conciudadanos!*" Monte threw down the gun; both hands grabbed his black locks and tugged with the ferocity of despair.

"Ah-h! What a lovely cuss-word," cried Jay. "How trippingly it goes upon the tongue. I must learn that. Say it again!"

"But eet ees not a bad word, that," said Monte sheepishly. "Eet ees onlee idle word, to feel up. When thees *politicos* go up an' down, talking nonsense een the nose, when they weesh to theenk of more, then they say with *emoción, 'O caballeros y conciudadanos'*; that ees, 'gentlemen and fellow ceetizens.' No more."

"Well, now, the story?" said Ben. "He crossed the river, going east—was that it?"

"Oh, yes. Well, when Numa Frenger see that thees gun ees emptee, he ees ver' angree man. He ees more enr-rage heemself for that than for all what gone befor-re. He ees ar-rouse all Belen, he ees send telegraph to Sabinal, La Joya, Socorro, San Marcial, ever wheech way, to meek queek the posse, to send queek to the mesa to catch thees man, to mek *proclamación* to pay for heem three thousand dollar of re-war-rd. 'Do not keel heem, I entr-reat you,' say Don Numa. 'Breeng heem back. I want to fry heem.' "

"Now isn't that New Mexico for you?" demanded Jay. "A man commits a barefaced robbery, and you make a joke of it."

Monte placed the middle finger of his right hand in the palm of his left, pressed firmly as if to hold something there, and looked up under his brows at Miss Hollister.

"Then why do you laugh?" said Monte.

"You win," said Jay. "Go on with the story."

"Well, then," said Monte, "thees fellow he go up on the high plain on thees side of the reever, and he ride east and south by Sierra Montoso, and over the mountains of Los Piños, and he mek to go over Chupadero Mesa to thoss ruins of Gran Quivira. But he ride onlee *poco á poco*, easalee. And already a posse from La Joya, San Acacia is ride up the Alamillo Cañon, and across the plain." His swift hands fashioned horseman, mountain, mesa, and plain. "Page Otero and six, five other men. And they ride veree fast so that already they pass in front of him to the south. They are now before heem on Chupadero, and there they see heem. Eet ees almost sundown.

"Inmediatamente he turn and go back. And their horses are not so tired lak hees horse, and they spread out and ride fast, and soon they are about to come weetheen gunshot weeth the rifle. And when he see eet, thees *colorado* ees ride oopon a reedge that all may see, and he tek that paper money from the nose bag at the head of the saddle and he toss eet up—pouf!

The weend is blow gentle and thees money it go joomp, joomp, here, there, een the booshes. Again he ride a leetle way, and again he scatter thees money lak a man to feed the hen een hees yard. So then he go on away, thees red one. And when thees posse come to that place, thees nize money is go hop, hop, along the ground and over the booshes. There ees feefty-dollar beel een the mesquite, there ees twenty-dollar beel een the tar-bush, there ees beels blow by, roll by, slide by. So thees posse ees dees-mount heemself to peek heem, *muy enérgico* —lively. And the weend ees come up faster at sundown, *como siempre* 'Come on!' says Page Otero. 'Come on, thees fellow weel to escape!' Then the posse loog up surprise, and say, 'Who, me?' and they go on to peek up thees monee. So that redhead get clear away thees time."

"Did they get all the money?" asked Ben.

"Numa he say yes. He do not know just how mooch thees bandit ees take, but he theenk they breeng back all, or most nearly all."

"Do they know who he was?" asked Jay.

"*Por cierto*, no. But from the deescreepcion and hees horse and saddle, they theenk eet ees a cowboy from Quemado, name—I cannot to pr-ronounce thees name, Meester Ben. You say heem. I have eet here een 'La Voz del Pueblo.' " From a hip pocket he produced a folded newspaper printed in Spanish, and showed Ben the place.

"Ross McEwen—about twenty-five or older, red hair, gray eyes, five feet nine inches—humph!" he returned the paper. "Will they catch him, do you think?"

Monte considered. He looked slowly at the far dim hills; he bent over to watch an inch-high horseman at his feet, toiling through painful immensities.

"The world ees ver' beeg een thees country," he said at last. "I theenk most mebbe not. *Quién sabe?* Onlee thees fellow must have water—and there ees not much water. Numa Frenger ees send now to all places, to Leencoln County; to Jeem Hunter here, and he meks every one to loog out; to Pat Garrett in Doña Ana

Countee, and Pat watches by Parker Lake and the pass of San Agustin; to El Paso, and they watch there most of all that he pass not to Mexico Viejo. Eet may be at some water place they get heem. Or that he get them. He seem lak a man of some enterpr-rize, no?" He rose to go. "But I have talk too much. I mus' go now to my beesness."

"A poor business for a man as bright as you are," said Jay, and sniffed.

"But I geeve a square deal," said Monte serenely. "Eet ees a good beesness. At your feet, señorita! Unteel then, Meester Ben."

"Isn't he a duck? I declare, it's a shame to laugh at his English," said Jay.

"Don't worry. He gets to hear our Spanish, even if he is too polite to laugh."

"I hate to think of that man being chased for blood money," said Jay. "Hunter and that Pat Garrett you think so much of are keen after that reward, it seems. It is dreadful the way these people here make heroes out of their killers and man-hunters."

"Let's get this straight," said Ben. "You're down on the criminal for robbing and down on the sheriff for catching him. Does that sound like sense? If there was no reward offered, it's the sheriff's duty to catch him, isn't it? And if there is a reward, it's still his duty. The reward doesn't make him a man-hunter. Woman, you ain't right in your head. And as for Pat Garrett and some of these other old-timers —they're enjoying temporary immortality right now. They've become a tradition while they still live. Do you notice how all these honest-to-goodness old-timers talk? All the world is divided into three parts. One part is old-timers and the other two are not. The most clannish people on earth. And that brings us, by graceful and easy stages, to the main consideration, which I want to have settled before I go. And when I say settled, I mean that nothing is ever settled till it is settled right—get me?" He stood up; as Jay rose he took both her hands. "If circumstances were otherwise, Jay?"

She avoided his eyes. "Don't ask me now. I

don't know, Ben—honest, I don't. You mustn't pester me now. It isn't fair when I'm so miserable." She pulled her hands away.

"Gawd help all poor sailors on a night like this!" said Ben fervently. "Listen, sister, I'm going to work, see? Goin' to fill your plans and specifications, every damn one, or bust a tug."

"I see you at it," jeered Jay, with an unpleasant laugh. "Work? You?"

"Me. I, myself. A faint heart never filled a spade flush," said Ben. "Going to get me a job and keep it. Lick any man that tries to fire me. Put that in your hope chest. Bye-bye, little didums. At your feet!"

As he went down the street his voice floated back to her:

> *"But now my hair is falling out,*
> *And down the hill we'll go,*
> *And sleep together at the foot—*
> *John Barleycorn, my Jo!"*

CHAPTER III

A HIGH broad tableland lies east of the Rio Grande, and mountains make a long unbroken wall to it, with cliffs that front the west. This mesa is known locally as El Corredor. It is a pleasing and wholesome country. Zacatón and salt grass are gray green upon the level plain, checkered with patches of bare ground, white and glaring. On those bare patches, when the last rains fell, weeks, months, or years ago, an oozy paste filmed over the glossy levels, glazed by later suns, cracking at last to shards like pottery. But in broken country, on ridges and slopes, was a thin turf of buffalo and mesquite grass, curly, yellow, and low. There was iron beneath this place and the sand of it was red, the soil was ruddy white, the ridges and the lower hill slopes were granite red, yellowed over with grass. Even the high crowning cliffs were faintly cream, not gray, as limestone is elsewhere. Sunlight was soft and mellow there, sunset was red upon these cliffs. And Ross McEwen fled down that golden corridor.

If he had ridden straight south, he might have been far ahead by this time, well on the road to Mexico. But his plan had been to reach the Panhandle of Texas; he had tried for easting and failed. Three times he had sought to work through the mountain barrier to the salt plains—a bitter country of lava flow and sinks, of alkali springs, salt springs, magnesia springs, soda springs; of soda lakes, salt lakes, salt marshes, salt creeks; of rotten and crumbling ground, of greasy sand, of chalk that powdered and rose on the lightest airs, to leave no trace that a fugitive had passed this way.

He had been driven back once by the posse on Chupadero. Again at night he had been

forced back by men who did not see him. He
had tried to steal through by the old Ozanne
stage road over the Oscuro, and found the pass
guarded; and the last time, to-day, had been
turned back by men that he did not even see.
In the mouth of Mockingbird Pass he had
found fresh-shod tracks of many horses going
east. Mockingbird was held against him.

He could see distinctly, and in one eye-
flight, every feature of a country larger than
all England. He could look north to beyond
Albuquerque, past the long ranges of Manzano,
Montoso, Sandia, Oscuro; southward, between
his horse's ears, the northern end of the San
Andrés was high and startling before him, blue
black with cedar brake and piñon, except for
the granite-gold top of Salinas Peak. West-
ward was the great valley of the Jornado del
Muerto, the Journey of the Dead, its width
the fifty miles which lay between the San
Andrés and the Rio Grande.

And beyond the river was a bright enor-
mous expanse, bounded only by the dozen

ranges that made the crest of the Continental Divide—Dátil, Magdalena, San Mateo, the Black Range, the Mimbres, Florida.

Between, bordering the midway river, other mountain ranges lay tangled: Cuchillo Negro, Fra Cristobál, Sierra de los Caballos, Doña Ana, Robelero. It was over the summits of these ranges that he saw the Continental Divide.

Here was irony indeed. With that stupendous panorama outspread before him, he was being headed off, driven, herded! He cocked an eyebrow aslant at the thought, and spoke of it to his horse, who pricked back an ear in attention. He was a honey-colored horse, and his name was Miél; which is, by interpretation, Honey.

"Wouldn't you almost think, sweetness," said Ross McEwen in a plaintive drawl, "that there was enough elbow-room here to satisfy every reasonable man? And yet these lads are crowdin' me like a cop after an alley cat."

He sensed that an unusual effort was being made to take him, and he smiled—a little ruefully—at the reflection that the people at Mockingbird might well have been mere chance comers upon their lawful occasions, and with no designs upon him, no knowledge of him. Every man was a possible enemy. He was out of law.

This was the third day of his flight. The man was still brisk and bold, the honey-colored horse was still sturdy, but both lacked something of the sprightly resilience they had brought to the fords of Belen. There had been brief grazing and scant sleep, night riding, doubling and twisting to slip into lonely water holes. McEwen had chosen, as the lesser risk, to ride openly to Prairie Springs. He had found no one there and had borrowed grub for himself and several feeds of corn for the Honey horse. There had been no fast riding, except for the one brief spurt with the posse on Chupadero. But it had been a steady grind, doubly tiresome that they might not keep to the beaten trails. Cross-country traveling on soft ground is rough on horseflesh.

And now they left the plain and turned through tar-bush up the long slope to the San Andrés. A thousand ridges and hollows came plunging and headlong against them; and with that onset, at once and suddenly the tough little horse was tiring, failing.

Halfway to the hill foot they paused for a brief rest. High on their slim lances, banners of yucca blossoms were white and waxen, and wild bees hummed to their homes in the flower stalks of last year; flaunting afar, cactus flowers flamed crimson or scarlet through the black tar-bush.

Long since McEwen had given up the Panhandle. He planned now to bear far to the southeast, crossing the salt plains below the White Sands to the Guadalupe Mountains, where they straddled the boundary between the territory and Texas, and so east to the Staked Plains. He knew the country ahead, or had known it ten years before. But there would be changes. There was a new railroad, so he had heard, from El Paso to Tularosa, and so

34

working north toward the States. There would
be other things, too—new ranches, and all that.
For sample, behind him, just where this long
slope merged with the flats, three unexpected
windmills, each five miles from the other, had
made a line across his path; he had made a
weary détour to pass unseen.

The San Andrés made here a twenty-mile
offset where they joined the Oscuro, with the
huge round mass of Salinas Peak as their mu-
tual corner. Lava Gap, the meeting-place of
the two ranges, was now directly at his left and
ten miles away. The bleak and mile-high walls
of it made a frame for the tremendous picture
of Sierra Blanca, sixty long miles to the east,
with a gulf of nothingness between. Below that
nothingness, as McEwen knew, lay the black
lava river of the Mal Pais. But Lava Gap was
not for him. Unless pursuit was quite abandoned, Lava Gap and Dripping Springs would
be watched and guarded. He was fenced in by
probabilities.

But the fugitive was confident yet, and by no

means at the end of his resources. He knew a dim old Indian trail over a high and improbable pass beyond Salinas Peak. It started at Grapevine Spring, Captain Jack Crawford's ranch.

"And at Grapevine," said Ross aloud, "I'll have to buy, beg, borrow, or get me a horse. Hope there's nobody at home. If there's any one there I'll have to get his gun first and trade afterwards. Borrowing horses is not highly recommended, but it beats killing 'em."

To the right and before him the Jornado was hazy, vast, and mysterious. To the right and behind him, the lava flow of San Pascual sprawled black and sinister in the lowlands; and behind him ——— Far behind him, far below him, a low line of dust was just leaving the central windmill of those three new ranches, a dozen miles away. McEwen watched this dust with some interest while he rolled and lit a cigarette. He drank the last water from his canteen.

"Come on, me bold outlaw," he said, "keep moving. You've done made your bed, but these hellhounds won't let you sleep in it." He put foot to stirrup; he stroked the Honey horse.

"Miél, old man, you tough it out four or five miles more, and your troubles will be over. Me for a fresh horse at Grapevine, come hell or high water. Take it easy. No hurry. Just shuffle along."

The pursuing dust did not come fast, but it came straight his way. "I'll bet a cooky," said Ross sagely, "that some of these gay bucks have got a spyglass. Wonder if that ain't against the rules? And new men throwin' in with them at every ranch. Reckon I would, too, if it wasn't for this red topknot of mine. Why couldn't they meet up with some other redheaded hellion and take him back? Wouldn't that be just spiffin"? One good thing, anyway—I didn't go back to the Quemado country. Some of the boys would sure have got in Dutch, hidin' me out. This is better."

He crossed the old military road that had once gone through Lava Gap to Fort Stanton; he smiled at the shod tracks there; he came to the first hills, pleasingly decorated with bunches of mares—American mares, gentle mares—Corporal Tanner's mares. He picked a bunch with four or five saddle horses in it and drove them slowly up Grapevine Cañon. The Miél horse held up his head and freshened visibly. He knew what this meant. The sun dropped behind the hills. It was cool and fresh in Grapevine.

The outlaw took his time. He had a long hour or more. He turned for a last look at the north and the cliffs of Oscuro Mountain blazing in the low sun to fiery streamers of red light. You would have seen, perhaps, only a howling wilderness; but this man was to look back, waking and in dream, and to remember that brooding and sunlit silence as the glowing heart of the world. From this place alone he was to be an exile.

"Nice a piece of country as ever laid outdoors," said Ross McEwen. "I've seen some several places where it would be right pleasant to have a job along with a bunch of decent punchers—good grub and all that, mouth organ by the firelight after supper————Or herding sheep."

Grapevine Spring is at the very head of the cañon. To east, south, and west the hills rise directly from the corral fences. McEwen drove the mares into the water pen and called loudly to the house. The hail went unanswered. Eagles screamed back from a cliff above him.

"A fool for luck," said McEwen.

He closed the bars, he gave Miél his first installment of water. Then he went to the house. It was unlocked and there was no one there. The ashes on the hearth were cold. He borrowed two cans of beans and some bacon; he borrowed and ground a little coffee. There was a slender store of corn, and he borrowed one feed of this to make to-morrow's breakfast for the new horse he was soon to acquire. He found an old saddle and he borrowed that, with an old bridle as well; he brought his own to replace them; he lit the little lamp on the table and grinned happily.

W. H. D. Koerner (1878–1938)

The pursuing dust did not come fast, but it came
straight his way.

"They'll find Miél and my saddle and the light," he said, "and they'll make sure I've taken to the brush."

He went back to the pen, he roped and saddled a saddle-marked brown, broad-chested and short-coupled, unshod. Shod tracks are too easily followed. Then he scratched his red head and grinned again. The pen was built of poles laid in panels, except at the front; the cedar brake grew to the very sides of it. He went to the back and took down two panels, laying the poles aside; he let the mares drift out there, seeing to it that some of them went around by the house, and the rest on the other side of the pen. It was almost dark by now.

"There," he said triumphantly. "The boys will drive in a bunch of stock when they come, for remounts, and they'll go right on through. Fine mess in the dark. And it'll puzzle them to find which way I went, with all these here tracks. Time I was gone."

He came back to the watering-trough; he washed his hands and face and filled his canteen; he went on where Miél stood weary and huddled in the dusk. His hand was gentle on that drooping neck.

"Miél, old fellow," he said, "you've been one good little horse to me. *Bueno suerte*." He led the brown to the bars. "I hate a fool," said Ross McEwen.

He took down the bars and rode into the cedar brush at right angles to the cañon, climbing steadily from the first. It was a high and desperate pass, and branches had grown across the unused trail; long before he had won halfway to the summit he heard, far below him, the crashing of horses in the brush, the sound of curses and laughter. The pursuit had arrived at Grapevine.

He topped the summit of that nameless pass an hour later, and turned down the dark cañon to the east—to meet grief at once. Since his time a cloudburst had been this way. Where once had been fair footing the flood had cut deep and wide, and every semblance of soil had washed away, leaving only a wild moraine, a loose rubble of rocks and tumbled boulders. But it was the only way. The hillsides were impossibly steep and sidelong, glassy granite and gneiss, or treacherous slides of porphyry. Ross led his horse. Every step was a hazard in that narrow and darkened place, with crumbling ridge and pit and jump off, with windrows of smooth round rock to roll and turn under their feet. It took the better part of two hours to win through the narrows, perhaps two miles. The cañon widened then, the hillsides were lower and Ross could ride again, picking his doubtful way in the starlight. He turned on a stepladder of hills to the north, and came about midnight to Dripstone, high in a secret hollow of the hills. The prodigious bulk of Salinas loomed mysterious and incredible above him in the starlight.

He tied the brown horse securely and named him Porch Climber. He built a tiny fire and toasted strips of bacon on the coals; he opened and ate one can of his borrowed beans. Then he spread out his saddle blankets with hat and saddle for pillow, and so lay down to untroubled sleep.

CHAPTER IV

HE awoke in that quiet place before the first stirring of dawn. A low thin moon was in the sky and the mountains were dim across the east. He washed his eyes out with water from the canteen. He made a nose bag from the corn sack and hung it on Porch Climber's brown head. The Belen nose bag had gone into the discard days before. He washed out the empty bean can for coffee-pot. He built a fire of twigs and hovered over it while his precious coffee came to a boil; his coat was thin and the night air was fresh, almost chilly. He smacked his lips over the coffee; he saddled and watered Porch Climber at Dripstone and refilled his canteen there. Porch Climber drank sparingly.

"Better fill up, old-timer," Ross advised him. "You're sure going to need it."

Knuckled ridges led away from Salinas like fingers of a hand. The eastern flat was some large fraction of a mile nearer to sea level than the high plain west of the mountain, and these ridges were massive and steep accordingly. He made his way down one of them. The plain was dark and cold below him; the mountains took shape and grew, the front range of the Rockies—Capitan, Carrizo, Sierra Blanca, Sacramento, with Guadalupe low and dim in the south; the White Sands were dull and lifeless in the midway plain. Bird twitter was in the air. Rabbits scurried through the brush, a quail whirred by and sent back a startled call; crimson streaks shot up the sky, and day grew broad across the silent levels. The cutbanks of Salt Creek appeared, wandering away southeast toward the marshes. Low and far against the black base of the Sacramento, white feathers lifted and fluffed, the smoke of the first fires at

Tularosa, fifty miles away. Flame tipped the far-off crests, the sun leaped up from behind the mountain wall, the level light struck on the White Sands, glanced from those burnished bevels and splashed on the western cliffs; the desert day blazed over this new half-world.

He had passed a few cows on the ridges, but now, as he came close to the flats, he was suddenly aware of many cattle before him, midges upon the vast plain; more cattle than he had found on the western side of the mountains. He drew rein, instantly on the alert, and began to quarter the scene with a keen scrutiny. At once a silver twinkling showed to northward —the steel fans of a windmill, perhaps six miles out from the foot of the main mountain. His eye moved slowly across the plain. He was shocked to find a second windmill tower some six or eight miles south of the first, keeping at the same distance from the hills, and when he made out the faint glimmer of a third, far in the south, he gave way to indignation.

It was a bald plain with no cover for the quietly disposed, except a few clumps of soapweed here and there. And this line of windmills was precisely the line of the road to El Paso. Where he had expected smooth going he would have to keep to the roughs; to venture into the open was to court discovery. He turned south across the ridges.

He had talked freely to Miél, but until now he had been reticent with Porch Climber, who had not yet won his confidence. At this unexpected reverse he opened his heart.

"Another good land gone wrong," he said. "I might have known it. This side of Salt Creek is only half-bad cow country, so of course it's all settled up, right where we want to go. Of course no one would live east of Salt Creek, not even sheep herders. And we couldn't possibly make it, goin' on the other side of Salt Creek with all that marsh country and the hell of the White Sands. Why, this is plumb ridiculous!"

He meditated for a while upon his wrongs

and then broke out afresh: "When I was here, the only water east of the mountains was the Wildy Well at the corner of the damn White Sands. Folks drove along the road, and when they wanted water they nicely went up in the hills. It's no use to cross over to Tularosa. They'll be waiting for us there. No, sir, we've pointedly got to skulk down through the brush. And you'll find it heavy going, up one ridge and down another, like a flea on a washboard."

Topping the next ridge, he reined back swiftly into a hollow place. He dismounted and peered through a mesquite bush, putting the branches aside to look. A mile to the south two horsemen paced soberly down a ridge—and it was a ridge which came directly from the pass to Grapevine.

"Now ain't them the bright lads?" said the runaway, divided between chagrin and admiration. "What are you going to do with fellows like that? I ask you. I left plain word that I done took to the hills afoot, without the shadow of a doubt. Therefore, they reasoned, I hadn't.

They've coppered every bet. Now that's what I call clear thinkin'. I reckon some of 'em did stay there, but these two crossed over that hellgate at night, just in case.

"I'll tell a man they had a ride where that cloudburst was. Say, they'll tell their grandchildren about that—if they live that long, which I misdoubt, the way they're carryin' on. This gives me what is technically known as the willies. Hawse," said McEwen, "let's us tarry a spell and see what these hirelin' bandogs are goin' to do now."

He took off the bridle and saddle, he staked Porch Climber to rest and graze while he watched. What the bandogs did was to ride straight to the central windmill, where smoke showed from the house. McEwen awaited developments. Purely from a sense of duty he ate the other can of beans while he waited.

"They'll take word to every ranch," he prophesied gloomily. "Leave a man to watch where there isn't any one there—take more men along when they find more than one at a well. Wish to God I was a drummer."

His prognostications were verified. After a long wait, which meant breakfast, a midget horseman rode slowly north toward the first windmill. A little later two men rode slowly south toward the third ranch.

"That's right, spread the news, dammit, and make everybody hate you," said Ross. He saddled and followed them, paralleling their course, but keeping to the cover of the brush.

It was heavy and toilsome going, boulders and rocks alternating with soft ground where Porch Climber's feet went through; gravel, coarse sand, or piled rocks in the washes; tedious twisting in the brush and wearisome windings where a bay of open country forced a détour. He passed by the mouths of Good Fortune, Antelope, and Cottonwood cañons, struggling through their dry deltas; he drew abreast of the northern corner of the White Sands. The reflection of it was blinding, yet he found it hard to hold his eyes away. The sun rode high and hot. McEwen consulted his canteen.

More than once or twice came the unwelcome thought that he might take to the hill country, discard Porch Climber and hide by some inaccessible seep or pothole until pursuit died down. But he was a stubborn man, and his heart was set upon Guadalupe; he had an inborn distaste for a diet of chance rabbit and tuna fruit—or, perhaps, slow deer without salt. A stronger factor in his decision—although he hardly realized it—was the horseman's hatred for being set afoot. He could hole up safely; there was little doubt of that. But when he came out of the hole, how then? A man from nowhere, on foot, with no past and no name and a long red beard—that would excite remark. He fingered the stubble on his cheeks with that reflection. Yes, such a man would be put to it to account for himself—and he would have to show up sometime, somewhere. The green cottonwood of Independent Spring showed high on the hill to his right. He held on to the south.

And now he came to the mouth of Sulphur Springs Cañon. Beyond here a great bay of open plain flowed into the hill foot under Kaylor Mountain; and midmost of that bay was another windmill, a long low house, spacious corrals. McEwen was sick of windmills. But this one was close under the mountain, far west of the line of the other ranches and of the El Paso road; McEwen saw with lively interest that his pursuers left the road and angled across the open to this ranch. That meant dinner.

"Honesty," said McEwen with conviction, "is the best policy. Dinner-time for some people, but only noon for me. . . . And how can these enterprisin' chaps be pursuin' me when they're in front? That isn't reasonable. Who ever heard of deputies goin' ahead and the bandit taggin' along behind? That's not right. It's not moral. I'm goin' around. Besides, if I don't this thing is liable to go on always, just windmills and windmills—to Mexico City— Peru—Chile. I'm plumb tired of windmills.

Porch Climber," said McEwen, "have you got any gift of speed? Because, just as soon as these two sheriff men get to that ranch and have time to go in the house, you and me are going to drift out quiet and unostentatious across the open country till we hit the banks of the Salt Marsh. And if these fellows look out and see us you've just got to run for it. They can maybe get fresh horses too. But if they don't see us we'll be right. We'll drift south under cover of the bank and get ahead of 'em while they stuff their paunches."

Half an hour later he turned Porch Climber's head to the east, and rode sedately across the smooth plain, desiring to raise no dust. Some three miles away, near where he crossed the El Paso road, grew a vigorous motte of mesquite trees. Once beyond that motte, he kept it lined up between him and the ranch; and so came unseen to where the plain broke away to the great marsh which rimmed the basin of the White Sands.

In the east the White Sands billowed in

great dry dunes above the level of the plain,
but the western half was far below that level,
and waterbound. This was the home of mi-
rages; they spread now all their pomp of palm
and crystal lake and fairy hill. McEwen turned
south along the margin. Here, just under the
bank, the ground was moist, almost wet, and
yet firm footing, like a road of hard rubber.
He brought Porch Climber to a long-reaching
trot, steady and smooth; he leaned forward
in his stirrups and an old song came to his lips,
unsummoned. He sang it with loving mockery,
in a nasal but not unpleasing baritone:

"They gave him his orders at Monroe, Virginia,
  Sayin', 'Pete, you're way behind ti-ime'———

"Gosh, it does seem natural to sing when a
good horse is putting the miles behind him,"
said McEwen. "This little old brown pony is
holdin' up right well, too, after all that grief
in the roughs this mawnin'.

"He looked 'raound then to his black,
   greasy fireman,
 'Just shovel in a little more co-o-al,

57

And when we cross that wide old maounting,
  You can watch old Ninety-Seven roll!'

"Hey, Porch Climber! You ain't hardly keepin' time. Peart up a little! Now, lemme see. Must be about twenty mile to the old Wildy Well. Wonder if I'll find any more new ranches between here and there? Likely. Hell of a country, all cluttered up like this!

"It's a mighty rough road from Lynchburg
    to Danville,
  And a line on a three-mile gra-ade,
It was on that grade that he lo-ost his av'rage,
  And you see what a jump he made!"

He rejoined the wagon road where the White Sands thrust a long and narrow arm far to the west. The old road crossed this arm at the shoulder, a three-mile speedway. Out on the sands magic islands came and went and rose and sunk in a misty sea. But in the south, where the road climbed again to the plain, was the inevitable windmill—reality and no mirage.

McEwen followed the road in the posture of a man who had nothing to fear. He had outridden the rumor of his flight; he could come to this ranch with a good face. But he reined down to a comfortable jog. Those behind might overtake him close enough to spy him in this naked place. Jaunting easily, nearing the ranch where he belonged, a horseman was no object of suspicion; but a man in haste was a different matter.

There was no one at the ranch. The water was brackish and flat, but the two wayfarers drank thankfully. He could see no signs that any horses were watering there; he made a shrewd guess that the boys had taken the horses and gone up into the mountains for better grass and sweet water, or perhaps to get out of sight of the White Sands, leaving the flats to the cattle.

"Probably they just ride down every so often to oil the windmill," he said. "Leastways, I would. Four hundred square miles of lookin'-glass, three hundred and sixty-four days a year —no, thank you! My eyes are 'most out now."

JB was branded on the gateposts of the corral; JB was branded on the door. He found canned stuff on a shelf and a few baking-powder biscuits, old and dry. He took a can of salmon and filed it for future reference.

"No time for gormandizin' now," he said. He stuffed the stale biscuits into his pocket to eat on the road. "There's this much about bread," said McEwen; "I can take it or I can leave it alone. And I've been leaving it alone for some several days now."

A pencil and a tablet lay on the table. His gray eyes went suddenly adance with impish light. He tore out a page and wrote a few words of counsel and advice:

> Hey, you JB waddies: Look out for a fellow with red hair and gray eyes. Medium-sized man. He robbed the bank at Belen, and they think he came this way. Big reward offered for him. Two thousand, I hear. But I don't know for certain. Send word to the ranches up north. I will tell them as far south as Organ.
>
> JIM HUNTLEY

He hung this news-letter on a nail above the stove.

"There!" he said. "If them gay jaspers that are after me had any sense a-tall, they'd see it was no use to go any further, and they'd stay right here and rest up. But they won't. They'll say, 'Hey, this is the way he went—here's some more of the same old guff! But how ever did that feller get down here without us findin' any tracks? You can see what a jump he made.' I don't want to be ugly," said McEwen, "but I've got to cipher up some way to shake loose from these fellows. I want to go to sleep. . . . Now who in hell is Jim Huntley?"

Time for concealment was past. From now on he must set his hope on speed. He rode down the big road boldly and, for a time, at a brisk pace; he munched the dry biscuits and washed them down with warm and salty water from his canteen.

There was hardly room for another ranch between here and Wildy's Well. Wildy's was an old established ranch. It was among the possibilities that he might hit here upon some old acquaintance whose failing sight would not note his passing, and who would give him a fresh horse. He was now needing urge of voice and spur for Porch Climber's lagging feet. It sat in his mind that Wildy was dead. His brows knitted with the effort to remember. Yes, Wildy had been killed by a falling horse. Most likely, though, he would find no one living at the well. Not too bad, the water of Wildy's Well— but they would be in the hills with the good grass.

The brown horse was streaked with salt and sweat; he dragged in the slow sand. Here was a narrow, broken country of rushing slopes, pinched between the White Sands and the mountains. The road wound up and down in the crowding brush; the footing was a coarse pebbly sand of broken granite from the crumbling hills. Heat waves rose quivering, the White Sands lifted and shuddered to a blinding shimmer, the dream islands were wavering, shifting, and indistinct, astir with rumor. McEwen's eyes were dull for sleep, red-rimmed and swollen from glare and alkali dust. The salt water was bitter in his belly. The stubble on his face was gray with powdered dust and furrowed with sweat stains; dust was in his nostrils and his ears, and the taste of dust was in his mouth. Porch Climber ploughed heavily. And all at once McEwen felt a sudden distaste for his affair.

He had a searching mind and it was not long before he found a cause. That damn song! Dance music. There were places where people danced, where they would dance to-night. There was a garden in Rutherford——

CHAPTER V

THERE was no one at Wildy's Well, no horses there and no sign that any horses were using there. McEwen drank deep of the cool sweet water. When Porch Climber had his fill, McEwen plunged arms and head into the trough. Horse and man sighed together; their eyes met in comfortable understanding.

"Feller," said McEwen, "it was that salt water, much as anything else, that slowed yuh up, I reckon. Yuh was sure sluggish. And yuh just ought to see yourself now! Nemmine, that's over." He took down his rope and cut off a length, the spread of his arms. He untwisted this length to three strands, soaked these strands in the trough, wrung them out and knotted them around his waist. He eyed the cattle that had been watering here. They had retreated to the far side at his coming and were now waiting impatiently. "Been many a long year since I've seen any Durham cattle," said McEwen. "Everybody's got white-face stuff now. Reckon they raise these for El Paso market. No feeder will buy 'em, unless with a heavy cut in the price."

He hobbled over and closed the corral gate. Every bone of him was a separate ache. A faint breeze stirred; the mill sails turned lazily; the gears squeaked a protest. Ross looked up with interest.

"That was right good water," he said. "Guess you've earned a greasing." He climbed the tall tower. Wildy's Well dated from before the steel windmill; this was massive and cumbersome, a wooden tower, and the wheel itself was of wood. After his oiling Ross scanned the north with an anxious eye. There was no dust. South by east, far in the central plain, dim hills swam indeterminate through the heat haze—Las Cornudas and Heuco. South by west, gold and rose, the peaks of the Organs peered from behind the last corner of the San Andrés. He searched the north again. He could see no dust—but he could almost see a dust. He shook his head. "Them guys are real intelligent," he said. "I'm losin' my av'rage." He clambered down with some celerity, and set about what he had to do.

He tied the severed end of his rope to the saddle horn, tightened the cinches, swung into the saddle, and shook out a loop. Hugging the fence, the cattle tore madly around the corral in a wild cloud of dust. McEwen rode with them on an inner circle, his eye on a big roan steer, his rope whirling in slow and measured rhythms. For a moment the roan steer darted to the lead; the loop shot out, curled over, and tightened on both forefeet; Porch Climber whirled smartly to the left; the steer fell heavily. Ross swung off; as he ran, he tugged at the hogging string around his waist. Porch

Climber dragged valiantly, Ross ran down the rope, pounced on the struggling steer, gathered three feet together and tied them with the hogging string. These events were practically simultaneous.

McEwen unsaddled the horse. "I guess you can call it a day," he said. He opened the gate and let the frightened cattle run out. "Here," he said, "is where I make a spoon or spoil a horn." He cut a thong from a saddle string and tied his old plough-handle forty-five so that it should not jolt from the scabbard. He made a tight roll of the folded bridle, that lonely can of salmon, and his coat, with his saddle blanket wrapped around all; he tied these worldly goods securely behind the cantle. He uncoupled the cinches and let out the quarter straps to the last hole.

The tied steer threshed his head madly, bellowing wild threats of vengeance. McEwen carried the saddle and placed it at the steer's back, where he lay. He found a short and narrow strip of board, like a batten, under the

68

tower; and with this, as the frantic roan steer heaved and threshed in vain efforts to rise, he poked the front cinch under the struggling body, inches at a time, until at last he could reach over and hook his fingers into the cinch ring. Before he could do this he was forced to tie the free foot to the three that were first tied; it had been kicking with so much fury and determination that the task could not be accomplished. Into the cinch ring he tied the free end of his rope, bringing it up between body and tied feet; he took a double of loose rope around his hips, dug his heels into the sand and pulled manfully every time the steer floundered; and so, at last and painfully, drew the cinch under until the saddle was on the steer's back and approximately where it should be. Then he put in the latigo strap, taking two turns, and tugged at the latigo till the saddle was pulled to its rightful place. At every tug the roan steer let out an agonized bawl. Then he passed the hind cinch behind the steer's hips and under the tail, drawing it up tightly so that the saddle could not slip over the steer's withers during the subsequent proceedings.

McEwen stood up and mopped the muddy sweat from his face; he rubbed his aching back. He filled his canteen at the trough, drank again, and washed himself. He rolled a smoke; he lashed the canteen firmly to the saddle forks. Porch Climber was rolling in the sand. McEwen took him by the forelock and led him through the open gate.

"If you should ask me," he said, "this corral is a spot where there is going to be trouble, and no place at all for you." He looked up the north road. Nothing in sight.

He went back to the steer. He hitched up his faded blue overalls, tightened his belt, and squinted at the sun; he loosened the last-tied foot and coiled the rope at the saddle horn. Then he eased gingerly into the saddle. The steer made lamentable outcry, twisting his neck in a creditable attempt to hook his tormentor; the free foot lashed out madly. But McEwen flattened himself and crouched safely, with a

full inch of margin; the steer was near to hook-
ing his own leg and kicking his own face, and
he subsided with a groan. McEwen settled himself in the saddle.

"Are ye ready?" said McEwen.

"Oi am!" said McEwen.

"Thin go!" said McEwen, and pulled the
hogging string.

The steer lurched sideways to his feet, paused
for one second of amazement, and left the
ground. He pitched, he plunged, he kicked at
the stirrups, he hooked at the rider's legs, he
leaped, he ran, bawling his terror and fury to
the sky; weaving, lunging, twisting, he crashed
sidelong into the fence, fell, scrambled up in an
instant. The shimmy was not yet invented.
But the roan steer shimmied, and he did it
nobly; man and saddle rocked and reeled.
Then, for the first time, he saw the open gate
and thundered through it, abandoning all
thought except flight.

Shaken and battered, McEwen was master.
The man was a rider. To use the words of a

later day, he was "a little warm, but not at all astonished." Yet he had not come off scot-free. When they crashed into the fence he had pulled up his leg, but had taken an ugly bruise on the hip. The whole performance, and more particularly the shimmy feature, had been a poor poultice for aching bones. Worse than all, the canteen had been crushed between fence and saddle. The priceless water was lost.

His hand still clutched the hogging string; he had no wish to leave that behind for curious minds to ponder upon. Until his mount slowed from a run to a pounding trot, he made no effort to guide him, the more because the steer's chosen course was not far from the direction in which McEwen wished to go. Wildy's Well lay at the extreme southwestern corner of the White Sands, and McEwen's thought was to turn eastward. He meant to try for Luna's Wells, the old stage station in the middle of the desert, on the road which ran obliquely from Organ to Tularosa. When time was ripe McEwen leaned over and slapped his hat into the steer's face, on the right side, to turn him to the left and to the east.

The first attempt at guidance, and the fourth attempt, brought on new bucking spells. McEwen gave him time between lessons; what he most feared was that the roan would "sull," or balk, refusing to go farther. When the steer stopped, McEwen waited until he went on of his own accord; when his progress led approximately toward McEwen's goal, he was allowed to go his own way unmolested. McEwen was bethorned, dragged through mesquite bushes, raked under branches; his shirt was ribboned and torn. But he had his way at last. With danger, with infinite patience, and with good judgment, he forced his refractory mount to the left and ever to the left, and so came at last into a deep trail which led due east. Muttering and grumbling, the steer followed the trail.

All this had taken time, but speed had also been a factor. When McEwen felt free to turn his head, only a half-circle of the windmill fans showed above the brush. Wildy's Well was miles behind them.

"Boys," said McEwen, "if you follow me this time, I'll say you're good!"

The steer scuffed and shambled, taking his own gait; he stopped often to rest, his tongue hung out, foam dripped from his mouth. McEwen did not urge him. The way led now through rotten ground and alkali, now through chalk that powdered and billowed in dust; deep trails, channeled by winds at war. As old trails grew too deep for comfort, the stock had made new ones to parallel the old; a hundred paths lay side by side.

McEwen was a hard case. A smother of dust was about him, thirst tormented him, his lips were cracked and bleeding, his eyes sunken, his face fallen in; and weariness folded him like a garment.

"Slate water is the best water," said McEwen.

They came from chalk and brush into a better country; poor, indeed, and starved, but the air of it was breathable. The sun was low and the long shadows of the hills reached out into the plain. And now he saw, dead in front, the gleaming vane and sails of a windmill. Only the top—the fans seemed to touch the ground—and yet it was clear to see. McEwen plucked up heart. This was not Luna's. Luna's was far beyond. This was a new one. If it stood in a hollow place—And it did!—It could not be far away. Water!

For the first time McEwen urged his mount, gently, and only with the loose and raveled tie string. Once was enough. The roan steer stopped, pawed the ground, and proclaimed flat rebellion. For ten minutes, perhaps, McEwen sought to overrule him. It was of no use. The roan steer was done. He took down his rope. With a little loop he snared a pawing and rebellious forefoot. He pulled up rope and foot with all his failing strength, and took a quick turn on the saddle horn. The roan made one hop and fell flat-long. McEwen tied three feet, though there was scant need for it. He took off the saddle, carried it to the nearest thicket and raised it, with pain, into the forks of a high soapweed, tucking up latigos and cinches. With pain; McEwen, also, was nearly done.

"My horse gave out on me. I toted my saddle a ways, but it was too heavy, and I hung it up so the cows couldn't eat it," he said, in the tone of one who recites a lesson.

He untied the steer then and came back hotfoot to his soapweed, thinking that the roan might be in fighting humor. But the roan was done. He got unsteadily to his feet, with hanging head and slavering jaws; he waited for a little and moved slowly away.

"Glad he didn't get on the prod," said McEwen. "I sure expected it. That was one tired steer. He sure done me a good turn. Guess I'll be strollin' into camp."

It was a sorry strolling. A hundred yards— a quarter—a half—a mile. The windmill grew taller; the first night breeze was stirring; he could see the fans whirl in the sun. A hundred yards—a quarter—a mile! An hour was gone. The shadows overtook him, passed him; the hills behind were suddenly very close and near, notched black against a crimson sky. Thirst tortured him, the windmill beckoned, sunset winds urged him on. He came to the brow of the shallow dip in which the ranch lay; he saw a little corral, a water pen, a long dark house beyond; he climbed into the water pen and plunged his face into the trough.

The windmill groaned and whined with a dismal clank and grinding of dry gears. Yet there was a low smoke over the chimney. How was this? The door stood open. Except for the creaking plaint of the windmill, a dead quiet hung about the place, a hint of something ominous and sinister. Stumbling, bruised, and outworn, McEwen came to that low dark door. He heard a choking cough, a child's wailing cry. His foot was on the threshold.

"What's wrong? *Que es?*" he called.

A cracked and feeble voice made an answer

77

W. H. D. Koerner (1878–1938)

He heard a choking cough, a child's wailing cry.
His foot was on the threshold. "What's wrong?
Que es?" he called.

that he could not hear. Then a man appeared at the inner door; an old man, a Mexican, clutching at the wall for support.

"El garrotillo," said the cracked voice. "The strangler—diphtheria."

"I'm here to help you," said McEwen.

CHAPTER VI

OF what took place that night McEwen had never afterward any clear remembrance, except of the first hour or two. The drone of bees was in his ears, and a whir of wings. He moved in a thin, unreal mist, giddy and light-headed, undone by thirst, weariness, loss of sleep—most of all by alkaline and poisonous dust, deep in his lungs. In the weary time that followed, though he daily fell more and more behind on sleep and rest, he was never so near to utter collapse as on this first interminable night. It remained for him a blurred and distorted vision of the dreadful offices of the sick-room; of sickening odors; of stumbling from bed to

bed as one sufferer or another shook with par-
oxysms of choking.

Of a voice, now far off and now clear, insistent with counsel and question, direction and
appeal; of lamplight that waned and flared
and dwindled again; of creak and clang and
pounding of iron on iron in horrible rhythm,
endless, slow, intolerable. That would be the
windmill. Yes, but where? And what windmill?

Of terror, and weeping, and a young child
that screamed. That woman—why, they had
always told him grown people didn't take diphtheria. But she had it, all right. Had it as bad
as the two youngsters, too. She was the mother,
it seemed. Yes, Florencio had told him that.
Too bad for the children to die. . . . But who
the devil was Florencio? The windmill turned
dismally—clank and rattle and groan.

That was the least one choking now—Felix.
Swab out his throat again. Hold the light. Care-
ful. That's it. Burn it up. More cloth, old man.
Hold the light this way. There, there, *pobre-*

cito! All right now. . . . Something was lurking in the corners, in the shadows. Must go see. Drive it away. What's that? What say? Make coffee? Sure. Coffee. Good idea. Salty coffee. Windmill pumpin' salt water. Batter and pound and squeal. Round and round. Round and round. Round and round. . . . Tell you what. Goin' to grease that damn windmill. Right now. . . . Huh? What's that? Wait till morning? All right. All ri'. Sure.

His feet were leaden. His arms minded well enough, but his hands were simply wonderful. Surprisin' skillful, those hands. How steady they were to clean membranes from little throats. Clever hands! They could bring water to these people, too, lift them up and hold the cup and not spill a drop. They could sponge off hot little bodies when the children cried out in delirium. Wring out rag, too! Wonderful hands! Mus' call people's 'tention to these hands sometime. There, there, let me wash you some more with the nice cool water. Now, now —nothing will hurt you. Uncle Happy's goin' to be right here, takin' care of you. Now, now —go to sleep—go-o to sleep!

But his feet were so big, so heavy and so clumsy, and his legs were insubordinate. 'Specially the calves. The calf of each leg, where there had once been good muscles of braided steel, was now filled with sluggish water of inferior quality. That wasn't the worst, either. There was a distinct blank place, a vacuum, something like the bead in a spirit level, and it shifted here and there as the water sloshed about. Wonder nobody had ever noticed that.

Must be edgin' on toward morning. Sick people are worst between two and four, they say. And they're all easier now, every one. Both kids asleep—tossin' about! And now the mother was droppin' off. Yes, sir—she's goin' to sleep. What did the old man call her? Estefanía. Yes —Est'fa'———

He woke with sunlight in his eyes. His arm sprawled before him a pine table and his head lay on his arm. He raised up, blinking,

84

and looked around. This was the kitchen, a sorry spectacle. The sick-room lay beyond an open door. He sat by that door, where he could see into the sick-room. They were all asleep. The woman stirred uneasily and threw out an arm. The old man lay huddled on a couch beyond the table.

McEwen stared. The fever had passed and his head was reasonably clear. He frowned, piecing together remembered scraps from the night before. The old man was Florencio Telles, the woman was the wife of his dead son, these were his grandchildren. Felix was one. Forget the other name. They had come back from a trip to El Paso a week ago, or some such matter, and must have brought the contagion with them. First one came down with the strangler, then another. Well poisoned with it, likely. Have to boil the drinking-water. This was called Rancho Perdido—the Lost Ranch. Well named. The old fellow spoke good English. McEwen was at home in Spanish, and, from

W. H. D. Koerner (1878–1938)

He sat by that door, where he could see into the
sick room. They were all asleep.

what he remembered of last night, the talk had been carried on in either tongue indifferently. What a night!

He rose and tiptoed out with infinite precaution. The wind was dead. He went to the well and found the oil; he climbed up and drenched the bearings and gears. He was surprised to see how weak he was and how sore; and for the first time in his life he knew the feeling of giddiness and was forced to keep one hand clutched tightly to some support as he moved around the platform—he, Ross Mc-Ewen.

When he came back the old man met him with finger on lip. They sat on the warm ground, where they could keep watch upon the sick-room, obliquely, through two doors; just far enough away for quiet speech to be unheard.

"Let them sleep. Every minute is so much of coined gold. We won't make a move to wake them. And how is it with you, my son?"

"Fine and fancy. When I came here last

night I had a thousand aches, and now I've got only one."

"And that one is all over?"

"That's the place. Never mind me. I'll be all right. How long has this been going on?"

"This is the fifth day for the oldest boy, I think. He came down with it first, Demetrio. We thought it was only a sore throat at first. Maybe six days. I am a little mixed up."

"Should think you would be. Now listen. I know something about diphtheria. Not much, but this for certain. Here's what you've got to do, old man: Quick as they wake up in there, you go to bed and stay in bed. You totter around much more and you're going to die. There's your fortune told, and no charge for it."

"Oh, I'm not bad. I do not cough hard. The strangler never hurts old people much." So he said, but every word was an effort.

"Hell, no, you're not bad. Just a walkin' corpse, tha's all. You get to bed and save your strength. When any two of 'em are chokin' to death at once, that'll be time enough for you

89

to hobble out and take one of them off my hands. Do they sleep this long, often?"

"Oh, no. This is the first time. They are always better when morning comes, but they have not all slept at the same time, never before. My daughter, you might say, has not slept at all. It has been grief and anxiety with her as much as the sickness. They will all feel encouraged now, since you've come. If it please God, we'll pull them all through."

"Look here!" said McEwen. "It can't be far to Luna's Well. Can't I catch up a horse and lope over there after while—bring help and send for a doctor?"

"There's no one there. Francisco Luna and Casimiro both have driven their stock to the Guadalupe Mountains, weeks ago. It has been too dry. And no one uses the old road now. All travel goes by the new way, beyond the new railroad."

"I found no one at the western ranches yesterday," said McEwen.

"No. Every one is in the hills. The drought

is too bad. There is no one but you. The nearest help is Alamogordo—thirty-five miles. And if you go there some will surely die before you get back. I have no more strength. I will be flat on my back this day."

"That's where you belong. I'll be nurse and cook for this family. Got anything to cook?"

"Not much. *Frijoles*, jerky, bacon, flour, a little canned stuff, and dried peaches."

McEwen frowned. "It is in my mind they ought to have eggs and milk."

"When the cattle come to water, you can shut up a cow and a calf—or two of them—and we can have a little milk to-night. I'll show you which ones. As I told you last night, I turned out the cow I was keeping up, for fear I'd get down and she would die here in the pen."

"Don Florencio, I'm afraid I didn't get all you told me last night," said McEwen thoughtfully. "I was wild as a hawk, I reckon. Thought that windmill would certainly drive me crazy. Fever."

The old man nodded. "I knew, my son. It galled my heart to make demands on you, but there was no remedy. It had to be done. I was at the end of my strength. Little Felix, if not the other, would surely have been dead by now, except for the mercy of God which sent you here."

McEwen seemed much struck by this last remark. He cocked his head a little to one side painfully, for his neck was stiff; he pursed his lip and held it between finger and thumb for a moment of meditation.

"So that was it!" he said. "I see! Always heard tell that God moves in a mysterious way His wonders to perform. I'll tell a man He does!"

A scanty breakfast, not without gratitude; a pitiful attempt at redding up the hopeless confusion and disorder. The sick woman's eyes followed McEwen as he worked. A good strangling spell all around, including the old man, then a period of respite. McEwen buckled on his gun and brought a hammer and a lard pail to Florencio's bed.

"If you need me, hammer on this, and I'll come a-running. I'm going out to the corral and shoot some beef tea. You tell me about what milk cows to shut up."

Don Florencio described several milk cows. "Any of them. Not all are in to water any one day. Stock generally come in every other day, because they get better grass at a distance. And my brand is TT—for my son Timoteo, who is dead. You will find the cattle in poor shape, but if you wait awhile you may get a smooth one."

McEwen nodded. "I was thinking that," he said. "I want some flour sacks. I'll hang some of the best up under the platform on the wind-mill tower, where the flies won't bother it."

They heard a shot later. A long time afterward he came in with a good chunk of meat, and set about preparing beef tea. "I shut up a cow to milk," he said. "A lot of saddle horses came in and I shut them up. Not any too much

93

water in the tank. After while the cattle will begin bawling and milling around, if the water's low. That will distress our family. Can't have that. So I'll just harness one on to the sweep of the horse power, slip on a blindfold, and let him pump. You tell me which ones will work."

The old man described several horses.

"That's O.K.," said McEwen. "I've got two of them in the pen. Your woodpile is played out. Had to chop down some of your back pen for firewood."

He departed to start the horse power. Later, when beef tea had been served all around, he came over and sat by Florencio's bed.

"You have no drop or grain of medicine of any kind," he said, "and our milk won't be very good when we get it, from the looks of the cows—not for sick people. So, everything being just as it is, I didn't look for brands. I beefed the best one I could find, and hung the hide on the fence. Beef tea, right this very now, may make all the difference with our family. Me,

94

I don't believe there's a man in New Mexico mean enough to make a fuss about it under the circumstances. But if there's any kick, there's the hide and I stand back of it. So that'll be all right. The brand was DW."

"It is my very good friend, Dave Woods, at San Nicolas. That will be all right. Don David is *muy simpático*. Sleep now, my son, sleep a little while you may. It will not be long. You have a hard night before you."

"I'm going up on the rising ground and set a couple of soapweeds afire," said McEwen at dark. "They'll make a big blaze and somebody might take notice. I'll hurry right back. Then I'll light some more about ten o'clock and do it again to-morrow night. Some one will be sure to see it. Just once, they might not think anything. But if they see a light in the same place three or four times, they might look down their nose and scratch their old hard head—a smart man might. Don't you think so?"

"Why, yes," said Florencio, "it's worth try-ing."

"Those boys are not a bit better than they was. And your daughter is worse. We don't want to miss a bet. Yes, and I'll hold a blanket before the fire and take it away and put it back, over and over. That ought to help people guess that it is a signal. Only—they may guess that it was meant for some one else."

"Try it," said Florencio. "It may work. But I am not sure that our sick people are not holding their own. They are no better, certainly, even with your beef-tea medicine. But we can't expect to see a gain, if there is a gain, for days yet. And so far, they seem worse every night and then better every morning. The sunlight cheers them up at first, and then the day gets hot and they seem worse again. Try your signals, by all means. We need all the help there is. But if you could only guess how much less alone I feel now than before you came, good friend!"

"It must have been plain hell!" said the good friend.

"Isn't there any other one thing we can do?" demanded McEwen the next day, cudgeling his brains. It had been a terrible night. The little lives fluttered up and down; Estefanía was certainly worse; Florencio, though he had but few strangling spells, was very weak—the aftermath of his earlier labors.

"Not one thing. My poor ghost, no man could have done more. There is no more to do."

"But there is!" McEwen fairly sprang up, wearied as he was. "We have every handicap in the world, and only one advantage. And we don't use that one advantage. The sun has a feud with all the damn germs there is; your house is built for shade in this hot country. I'm going to tote all of you out in the sun with your bedding, and keep you there a spell. And while you're there I'll tear out a hole in the south end of your little old adobe wall and let more sunlight in. After the dust settles enough, I'll bring you back. Then we'll shovel on a little more coal, and study up something else.

And to-night we'll light up our signal fires again. Surely some one will be just fool enough to come out and see what the hell it's all about."

Hours later, after this programme had been carried out, McEwen roused from a ten minute sleep and rubbed his fists in his eyes.

"Are you awake, Don Florencio?" he called softly.

"Yes, my son. What is it?"

"It runs in my mind," said McEwen, "that they burn sulphur in diphtheria cases. Now, if I was to take the powder out of my cartridges and wet it down, let it get partly dry and make a smudge with it—a little at a time——— There's sulphur in gunpowder. We'll try that little thing." He was already at work with horseshoe pinchers, twisting out the bullet. He looked up eagerly. "Haven't any tar, have you? To stop holes in your water troughs."

"*Hijo*, you shame me. There is a can of piñon pitch, that I use for my troughs, under the second trough at the upper end. I never once thought of that."

98

"We're getting better every day," said Mc-Ewen joyfully. "We'll make a smoke with some of that piñon wax, and we'll steep some of it in boiling water and breathe the steam of it; we'll burn my wet powder, and when that's done, we'll think of something else; and we'll make old bones yet, every damn one of us! By gollies, to-morrow between times I'm goin' to take your little old rifle and shoot some quail."

"Between times? Oh, Happy!"

"Oh, well, you know what I mean—just shovel on a little more coal—better brag than whine. Hi, Estefanía—hear that? We've dug up some medicine. Yes, we have. Ask Don Florencio if we haven't. I'm going after it."

As he limped past the window on his way to the corral he heard the sound of a sob. He paused midstep, thinking it was little Felix. But it was Estefanía.

"Madre de Dios, ayudale su enviado!"

He tiptoed away, shamefaced.

CHAPTER VII

SLEEPING on a very thin bed behind a very large boulder, two men camped at the pass of San Agustin; a tall young man and a taller man who was not so young. The very tall man was Pat Garrett, sheriff of Doña Ana, sometime sheriff of other counties. The younger man was Clint Llewellyn, his deputy, and their camp was official in character. They were keeping an eye out for that Belen bandit, after prolonged search elsewhere.

"Not but what he's got away long ago," said Pat, in his quiet, drawling speech, "but just in case he might possibly double back this way."

It was near ten at night when Pat saw the

light on the desert. He pointed it out to Clint. "See that fire out there? Your eyes are younger than mine. Isn't it sinking down and then flaring up again?"

"Looks like it is," said Clint. "I saw a fire there—or two of 'em, rather—just about dark, while you took the horses down to water."

"Did you?" said Pat. He stroked his mustache with a large slow hand. "Looks to me like some one was trying to attract attention."

"It does, at that," said Clint. "Don't suppose somebody's had a horse fall with him and got smashed, do you?"

"Do you know," said Pat slowly, "that idea makes me ache, sort of? One thing pretty clear. Somebody wants some one to do something for somebody. Reckon that's us. Looks like a long ride, and maybe for nothing. Yes. But then we're two long men. Where do you place that fire, Clint?"

"Hard to tell. Close to Luna's Wells, maybe."

"Too far west for that," said Garrett. "I'd

say it was Lost Ranch. We'll go ask questions, anyway. If we was layin' out there with our ribs caved in or our leg broke———Let's go!"

That is how they came to Lost Ranch between three and four the next morning. A feeble light shone in the window. Clint took the horses to water, while Garrett went on to the house. He stopped at the outer door. A man lay on a couch within, a man Garrett knew—old Florencio. Folded quilts made a pallet on the floor, and on the quilts lay another man, a man with red hair and a red stubble of beard. Both were asleep. Florencio's hand hung over the couch, and the stranger's hand held to it in a tight straining clasp. Garrett stroked his chin, frowning.

Sudden and startling, a burst of strangled coughing came from the room beyond and a woman's sharp call.

"*Hijo!*" cried Florencio feebly, and pulled the hand he held. "Happy! Wake up!" The stranger lurched to his feet and staggered

W. H. D. Koerner (1878–1938)

That is how they came to Lost Ranch between three
  and four the next morning.

through the door. "Yes, Felix, I'm coming. All right, boy! All right now! Let me see. It won't hurt. Just a minute, now."

Garrett went into the house.

"Clint," said Pat Garrett, "there's folks dyin' in there, and a dead man doin' for them. You take both horses and light a rag for the Alamogordo Hospital. Diphtheria. Get a doctor and nurses out here just as quick as God will let them come." Garrett was pulling the saddle from his horse as he spoke. "Have 'em bring grub and everything. Ridin' turn about, you ought to make it tolerable quick. I'm stayin' here, but there's no use of your comin' back. You might take a look around Jarilla if you want to, but use your own judgment. Drag it, now. Every minute counts."

A specter came to the doorway. "Better send a wagonload of water," it said as Clint turned to go. "This well is maybe poisoned. Germs and such."

"Yes, and bedding, too," said Clint. "I'll get everything and tobacco. So long!"

"Friend," said Pat, "you get yourself to bed. I'm takin' on your job. Your part is to sleep."

"Yes, son," Florencio's thin voice quavered joyously. "*Duerme y descansa.* Sleep and rest. Don Patricio will do everything."

McEwen swayed uncertainly. He looked at Garrett with stupid and heavy eyes. "He called you Patricio. You're not Pat Nunn, by any chance?"

"Why not?" said Garrett.

McEwen's voice was lifeless. "My father used to know you," he said drowsily. He slumped over on his bed.

"Who was your father?" said Garrett.

McEwen's dull and glassy eyes opened to look up at his questioner. "I'm no credit to him," he said. His eyes closed again. "Boil the water!" said McEwen.

"He's asleep already!" said Pat Garrett. "The man's dead on his feet."

"Oh, Pat, there was never one like him!" said Florencio. He struggled to his elbow, and looked down with pride and affection at the sprawling shape on the pallet. "Don Patricio, I have a son in my old age, like Abrahán!"

"I'll pull off his boots," said Pat Garrett.

Garrett knelt over McEwen and shook him vigorously. "Hey, fellow, wake up! You, Happy—come alive! Snap out of it! Most sundown, and time you undressed and went to bed."

McEwen sat up at last, rubbing his eyes. He looked at the big, kindly face for a little in some puzzlement. Then he nodded.

"I remember you now. You sent your pardner for the doctor. How's the sick folks?"

"I do believe," said Pat, "that we're going to pull 'em through—every one. You sure had a tough lay."

"Yes. Doctor come?"

"He's in sight now—him and the nurses. That's how come me to rouse you up. Feller, I hated to wake you when you was going so good. But with the ladies comin', you want to spruce yourself up a bit. You look like the wrath of God!"

McEwen got painfully to his feet and wriggled his arms experimentally.

"I'm just one big ache," he admitted. "Who's them fellows?" he demanded. Two men were industriously cleaning up the house; two men that he had never seen.

"Them boys? Monte, the Mexican, he's old Florencio's nephew. Heard the news this mawnin', and comes boilin' out here hell-for-leather. Been here for hours. The other young fellow came with him. Eastern lad. Don't know him, or why he came. Say, Mr. Happy, you want to bathe those two eyes of yours with cold water, or hot water, or both. They look like two holes burned in a blanket. Doc will have to give you a good jolt of whiskey, too. Man, you're pretty nigh ruined!"

"I knew there was something," said Mr. Happy. "Got to get me a name. And gosh, I'm tired! I'm a good plausible liar, most times, but

I'll have to ask you to help me out. Andy Hightower—how'd that do? Knew a man named
Alan Hightower once, over on the Mangas."

"Does he run cattle over there now somewhere about Quemado?"

"Yes," said McEwen.

"I wouldn't advise Hightower," said Garrett.

"My name," said McEwen, "is Henry Clay."

Dr. Lamb, himself the driver of the covered
spring wagon, reached Lost Ranch at sundown.
He brought with him two nurses, Miss Mason
and Miss Hollister, with Lida Hopper, who
was to be cook; also, many hampers and much
bedding. Dad Lucas was coming behind, the
doctor explained, with a heavy wagon, loaded
with water and necessaries. Garrett led the way
to the sick-room.

Monte helped Garrett unload the wagon and
care for the team; Lida Hopper prepared supper in the kitchen.

Mr. Clay had discreetly withdrawn, together
with the other man. They were out in the corral now, getting acquainted. The other man,

it may be mentioned, was none other than Ben Griggs; and his discretion was such that Miss Hollister knew nothing of his presence until the next morning.

Mr. Clay, still wearied, bedded down under the stars, Monte rustling the credentials for him. When Dad Lucas rolled in, the men made camp by the wagon.

"Well, doctor," said Garrett, "how about the sick? They are going to make it?"

"I think the chances are excellent," said the doctor. "Barring relapse, we should save every one. But it was a narrow squeak. That young man who nursed them through—why, Mr. Garrett, no one on earth could have done better, considering what he had to do with. Nothing, practically, but his two hands."

"You're all wrong there, doc. He had a backbone all the way from his neck to the seat of his pants. That man," said Garrett, "will do to take along."

"Where is he, Mr. Garrett? And what's his name? The old man calls him 'son,' and the boys call him 'Uncle Happy.' What's his right name?"

"Clay," said Garrett, "Henry Clay. He's dead to the world. You won't see much of him. A week of sleep is what he needs. But you remind me of something. If you will let me, I would like to speak to all of you together. Just a second. Would you mind asking the nurses to step in for a minute or two, while I bring the cook?"

"Certainly," said Dr. Lamb.

"I want to ask a favor of all of you," said Garrett, when the doctor had ushered in the nurses. "I won't keep you. I just want to declare myself. Some of you know me, and some don't. My name is Pat Garrett, and I am sheriff of Doña Ana County, over west. But for reasons that are entirely satisfactory to myself, I would like to be known as Pat Nunn, for the present. That's all. I thank you."

"Of course," said Dr. Lamb, "if it is to serve the purpose of the law———"

"I would not go so far," said Garrett. "If you put it that my purpose is served, you will be quite within the truth. Besides, this is not official. I am not sheriff here. This ranch is just cleverly over the line and in Otero County. Old Florencio pays taxes in Otero. I am asking this as a personal favor, and only for a few days. Perfectly simple. That's all. Thank you."

"Did you ask the men outside?"

"No. I just told them," said Mr. Pat Nunn. "It would be dishonorable for a lady to tip my hand; for a man it would be plumb indiscreet."

"Dad Lucas," said the doctor, "is a cynical old scoundrel, and a man without principle, and swivel-tongued besides."

"He is all that you say, and a lot more that you would never guess," said Garrett. "But if I claimed to be Humpty Dumpty, Dad Lucas would swear that he saw me fall off of the wall." He held up his two index fingers, side by side. "Dad and me, we're like that. We've seen trouble together—and there is no bond so close. Again, one and all, I thank you. Meetin's adjourned.

Lost Ranch was a busy scene on the following day. A cheerful scene, too, despite the blazing sun, the parched desert, and the scarred old house. Reports from the sick-room were hopeful. The men had spread a tarpaulin by the wagon, electing Dad Lucas for cook. They had salvaged a razor of Florencio's and were now doing mightily with it. Monte and Ben Griggs, after dinner, were to take Dad's team and Florencio's wagon to draw up a jag of mesquite roots; in the meantime Monte dragged up stop-gap firewood by the saddle horn, and Ben kept the horse power running in the water pen. Keeping him company, Pat Garrett washed Henry Clay's clothes. More accurately, it was Pat Nunn who did this needed work with grave and conscientious thoroughness.

"Henry Clay and me, after bein' in the house so long," said Mr. Nunn, "why, we'll have to boil up our clothes before we leave, or we might go scattering diphtheria hither and yonder and elsewhere."

"But how if you take it yourselves?"

"Then we'll either die or get well," said Mr. Nunn slowly. "In either case, things will keep juneing along just the same. Henry Clay ain't going to take it, or he'd have it now. It takes three days after you're exposed. Something like that. We'll stick around a little before we go, just in case."

"Which way are you going, Mr. Nunn?" asked Ben.

"Well, I'm going to Tularosa. Old Florencio will have to loan me a horse. Clay too. He's afoot. Don't know where he's going. Haven't asked him. He's too worn out to talk much. His horse played out on him out on the flat somewheres and he had to hang up his saddle and walk in. So Florencio told me. He's goin' back and get his saddle to-morrow."

Miss Mason being on duty, Jay Hollister, having picked up a bite of breakfast, was minded to get a breath of fresh air; and at this juncture she tripped into the water pen where Mr. Nunn and Ben plied their labors.

"And how is the workingman's bride this morning?" asked Ben brightly.

"Great Caesar's ghost! Ben Griggs, what in the world are you doing here?" demanded Jay with a heightened color.

"Workin'," said Ben, and fingered his blue overalls proudly. "Told you I was goin' to work. Right here is where I'm needed. Why, there are only four of us, not counting you three girls and the doctor, to do what this man Clay was doing. You should have seen Monte and me cleaning house yesterday."

"Yes?" Jay smiled sweetly. "What house was that?"

"Woman!" said Ben, touched in his workman's pride. "If you feel that way now, you should have seen this house when we got here."

"You're part fool. You'll catch diphtheria."

"Well, what about you? The diphtheria part, I mean. What's the matter with your gettin' diphtheria?"

"That's different. That's a trade risk. That's my business."

"You're my business," said Ben.

Jay shot a startled glance at Mr. Nunn, and shook her head.

"Oh, yes!" said Ben. "Young woman, have you met Mr. Nunn?"

Soap in hand, Mr. Nunn looked up from his task. "Good-morning, miss. Don't mind me," he said. "Go right on with the butchery."

"Good-morning, Mr. Nunn. Please excuse us. I was startled at finding this poor simpleton out here where he has no business to be. Have I met Mr. Nunn? Oh, yes, I've met him twice. The doctor introduced him once, and he introduced himself once."

Mr. Nunn acknowledged this gibe with twinkling eye. Miss Hollister looked around her, and shivered in the sun. "What a ghastly place!" she cried. "I can't for the life of me understand why anybody should live here. We came through some horrible country yesterday, but this is the worst yet. Honestly, Mr. Nunn, isn't this absolutely the most God-forsaken spot on earth?"

Mr. Nunn abandoned his work for the moment and stood up, smiling. So this was Pat Garrett of whom she had heard so much; the man who killed Billy the Kid. Well, he had a way with him. Jay could not but admire the big square head, the broad spread of his shoulders, and a certain untroubled serenity in his quiet face.

"Oh, I don't know," said Mr. Nunn. "Look there!"

"Where? I don't see anything," said Jay. "Look at what?"

"Why, the bees," said Pat. "The wild bees. They make honey here. Little family of 'em in every *sotol* stalk; and that old house up there with the end broken in——No, Miss Hollister, I've seen worse places than this."

CHAPTER VIII

THE patients were improving. Old Florencio, who had been but lightly touched, mended apace. He had suffered from exhaustion and distress quite as much as from disease itself. Demetrio and little Felix gained more slowly, and Estefanía was weakest of all. The last was contrary to expectation. As a usual thing, diphtheria goes hardest with the young. But all were in a fair way to recover. Dr. Lamb and Dad Lucas had gone back to town. Dad had returned with certain comforts and luxuries for the convalescents.

Jay Hollister, on the morning watch, was slightly annoyed. Mr. Pat Garrett and the man

Clay were leaving, it seemed, and nothing would do but that Clay must come to the sick-room for leave-taking. Quite naturally, Jay had not wished her charges disturbed. Peace and quiet were what they needed. But Garrett had been insistent, and he had a way with him. Oh, well! The farewell was quiet enough and brief enough on Clay's part, goodness knows, but rather fervent from old Florencio and his daughter-in-law. That was the Spanish of it, Jay supposed. Anyhow, that was all over and the disturbers were on their way to Tularosa.

Relieved by Miss Mason, Jay went in search of Ben Griggs to impart her grievance, conscious that she would get no sympathy there, and queerly unresentful of that lack. He was not to be seen. She went to the kitchen.

"Where's that trifling Ben, Lida?"

"Him? I'm sure I don't know, Miss Jay. That Mexican went up on top of the house just now. He'll know, likely."

Jay climbed the rickety ladder, stepped on the adobe parapet and so down to the flat roof.

Monte sat on the farther wall looking out across the plain so intently that he did not hear her coming.

"Do you know where Ben is?" said Jay.

Monte came to his feet. "Oh, yais! He is weeth the Señor Lucas to haul wood, Mees Hollister. Is there what I can do?"

"What are we going to do about water?" said Jay. "There's only one barrel left. Of course, we can boil the well water, but it's horrible stuff."

"*Prontamente*—queeckly. All set. Ben weel be soon back, and here we go, Ben and me, to the spreeng of San Nicolás." He pointed to a granite peak of the San Andrés. "There at thees peenk hill yonder."

"What, from way over there?"

"Eet ees closest, an ver' sweet water, ver' good."

Jay looked and wondered, tried to estimate the void that lay between, and could not even guess. "What a dreadful country! How far is it?"

"Oh, twent-ee miles. *Es nada.* We feel up by sundown and come back in the cool stars."

"Oh, do sit down," said Jay, "and put on your hat. You're so polite you make me nervous. I shouldn't think you'd care much about the cool," said Jay, "the way you sit up here, for pleasure, in the broiling sun."

"Plezzer? Oh, no!" said Monte. "Look!" He turned and pointed. "No, not here, not close by. Mebbe four, three miles. Look across thees bare spot an' thees streep of mesquite to thees long chalk reedge; and now, beyond thees row and bunches of yuccas. You see them now?"

Jay followed his hand and saw, small and remote, two horsemen creeping black and small against the infinite recession of desert. She nodded.

"Eet ees with no joy," said Monte, "that I am to see the las' of *un caballero valiente*—how do you say heem?—of a gallan' gentlemen—thees redhead."

"You are not very complimentary to Mr. Garrett," said Jay.

"Oh, no, no, no—you do not understand!" Monte's eyes narrowed with both pity and puzzlement. He groped visibly for words. *"Seguramente, siempre*, een all ways Pat Garrett ees a man complete. Eet is known. But thees young fellow—he ees play out the streeng—*pobrecito!* Oh, Mees Jay, eet ees a bad spread! Es-scusame, please, Mees Hollister. I have not the good words—onlee the man talk."

"Oh, he did well enough—but why not?" said Jay. "What else could he do? There has been something all the time that I don't understand. Danger from diphtheria? Nonsense. I am not a bit partial to you people out here. Perhaps you know that. But I must admit that danger doesn't turn you from anything you have set your silly heads to do. Of course Mr. Clay had to work uncommonly hard, all alone here. But he had no choice. No; it's something else, something you have kept hidden from me all along. Why all the conspiracy and the pussy-foot mystery?"

"Eet was not jus' lak that, mees. Not *conjuración* exactlee. But everee man feel for heemself eet ees ver' good to mek no talk of thees theeng." For once Monte's hands were still. He looked off silently at the great bare plain and the little horsemen dwindling in the distance. "I weel tell you, then," he said at last. "Thees *cosa* are bes' not spoken, and yet eet ees right for you shall know. Onlee I have not those right words. Ben, he shall tell you when he come."

Again he held silence for a little space, considering. "Eet ees lak thees, Mees Jay. Ver' long ago—yais, before not any of your people is cross over the Atlantic Ocean—my people they are here een thees country and they go up and down to all places—yais, to *las playas del mar*, to the shores of the sea by California. And when they go by Zuñi and by thees rock El Morro, wheech your people call—I have forget that name. You have heard heem?"

124

"Yes," said Jay. "Inscription Rock. I've read about it."

"*Si, si!* That ees the name. Well, eet ees good camp ground, El Morro, wood and water, and thees gr-reat cleef for shade and for shelter een estr-rong winds. And here some fellow he come and he cry out, "*Adiós, el mundo!* What lar-rge weelderness ees thees! And me, I go now eento thees beeg lonesome, and perhaps I shall not to r-return! *Bueno, pues*, I mek now for me a gravestone!" and so he mek on that beeg rock weeth hees dagger, "*Pasó por aquí, Don Fulano de Tal*"—passed by here, Meester So-and-So —weeth the year of eet.

"And after heem come others to El Morro— so few, so far from Spain. They see what he ees write there, and they say, '*Con razón!*'— eet ees weeth reason to do thees. An' they also mek eenscreepción, '*Pasó por aquí*'—and their names, and the year of eet."

His hand carved slow letters in the air. His eye was proud.

"I would not push my leetleness upon thees

so lar-rge world, but one of thees, Mees Hollister—oh, not of the great, not of the first—he was of mine, my ver' great, great papa. So long ago! And he mek also, '*Pasó por aquí*, Salvador Holguin.' I hear thees een the firelight when I am small fellow. And when I am man-high I mek veesit to thees place and see heem."

His eye followed the far horsemen, now barely to be seen, a faint moving blur along the north.

"And thees fellow, too, thees redhead, he pass this way, '*Paso por aqui*' "—again the brown hand wrote in the air—"and he mek here good and not weeked. But, before that—I am not God!" Lips, shoulders, hands, every line of his face disclaimed that responsibility. "But he is thief, I theenk," said Monte. "Yais, he ees thees one—Mack-Yune?—who rob the bank of Numa Frenger las' week at Belen. I theenk so."

Jay's eyes grew round with horror, her hand went to her throat. "Not arrested?"

For once Monte's serene composure was

shaken. His eyes narrowed, his words came headlong.

"O, no-no-no! You do not unnerstan'. Ees eemposevilly, what you say! Pat Garrett ees know nozzing, he ees fir-rm r-resolve to know nozzing. An' thees Mack-Yune, he ees theenk *por verdad* eet ees Pat Nunn who ride weeth heem to Tularosa. He guess not one theeng that eet ees the sheriff. Pat Garrett he go that none may deesturb or moless' heem. Becows, thees young fellow ees tek eshame for thees bad life, an' he say to heemself, 'I weel arize and go to my papa.' "

She began to understand. She looked out across the desert and the thorn, the white chalk and the sand. Sun dazzle was in her eyes. These people! Peasant, gambler, killer, thief——— She felt the pulse pound in her throat.

"And een Tularosa, all old-timers, everee man he know Pat Garrett. Not lak thees Alamogordo, new peoples. And when thees old ones een Tularosa see Meester Pat Garrett mek good-bye weeth hees friend at the tr-rain, they will theenk nozzing, say nozzing. *Adiós!*"

He sat sidewise upon the crumbling parapet and waved his hand to the nothingness where the two horsemen had been swallowed up at last.

"And him the sheriff!" said Jay. "Why, they could impeach him for that. They could throw him out of office."

He looked up smiling, "But who weel tell?" said Monte. His outspread hands were triumphant. "We are all decent people."

THE END